Unusual Plants of the Galaxy

Other book collections by Arthur Porges:

Three Porges Parodies and a Pastiche (1988)
The Mirror and Other Strange Reflections (2002)
Eight Problems in Space: The Ensign De Ruyter Stories (2008)
The Adventures of Stately Homes and Sherman Horn (2008)
The Calabash of Coral Island and Other Early Stories (2008)
The Miracle of the Bread and Other Stories (2008)
Spring, 1836: Selected Poems (2008)
The Devil and Simon Flagg and Other Fantastic Tales (2009)
The Curious Cases of Cyriack Skinner Grey (2009)
The Ruum and Other Science Fiction Stories (2010)
The Rescuer and Other Science Fiction Stories (2014)

Forthcoming titles by Arthur Porges:

The Price of a Princess: Hardboiled Crime Fiction
Collected Essays: Volume One
Collected Essays: Volume Two

Books by F. W. Thomas (from the same publisher):

Tales From Stonecutter Street (2010)
Star Turns (2011)
The Rising Sap (2013)

Unusual Plants of the Galaxy

Arthur Porges

Edited by Richard Simms

Richard Simms Publications

This paperback first edition published in 2014

Richard Simms Publications, Surrey, England

ISBN: 978-0-9930387-0-9

The seven "Unusual Plants of the Galaxy" articles collected in this volume first appeared in the periodical *Memo*, ca. 1996.

With special thanks to Cele Porges and Joel Hoffman.

For more information please visit The Arthur Porges Fan Site:

http://arthurporges.atwebpages.com

Contents

Introduction

Back in the mid-1990s, Arthur Porges took a break from writing poetry, a creative field in which he had been absorbed for the most part after retiring as a full-time author of short fiction. For some years only the odd short story had surfaced from time to time in periodicals such as *Alfred Hitchcock's Mystery Magazine*. Having gained the interest of the editor of a small, obscure journal called *Memo* (now defunct), Porges set about contributing his short-lived "Unusual Plants of the Galaxy" series to that publication; an intriguing body of work that has never been reprinted until now.

Drawing heavily on his interests in botany, astronomy, biology, and his love of nature in general, Porges, writing with detail and precision, skillfully coupled this knowledge base with a science fiction sensibility (a genre in which, incidentally, he had not written for decades) to conceive the "Unusual Plants of the Galaxy" sequence, which consists of the seven delightful pieces that make up this collection.

As they are in the form of vignettes, the writing is even tighter than usual for Porges. The briskly delineated descriptions of the fictitious plants the author has so deftly imagined are a masterclass in brevity.

Penning them for the sheer fun of it as much as anything else, one senses that in doing so Arthur was truly in his element. I know from our correspondence that he was fond of these, his personal favorite being "Vedius Flame-Lily," a startling, well-realized idea that half convinces the reader such an extraordinary organism could well exist somewhere among the distant stars.

So what we have here is fiction masquerading as fact; feature articles from a far future when mankind has explored space beyond the confines of our own solar system and visited distant planets many light years from Earth. And with the recent discovery via the *Kepler* telescope of hundreds of exoplanets orbiting other stars in our galaxy (with no doubt many thousands more waiting to be found), one cannot help thinking that Porges' speculations have even more resonance today. Just one of the possible wonders we may discover out there could well be certain bizarre manifestations of flora that have evolved in the alien environments of other worlds, such as those envisaged so vividly in the pieces assembled in this volume.

It is a pleasure to give this small but significant series the honor of preservation in book form, and of course to afford it a wider exposure. Enjoy!

Richard Simms
Surrey, England
July, 2014

Vedius Flame-Lily

The Flame-Lily of Vedius, the second planet of the blue supergiant Saiph, a 2.1 magnitude star 720 light years from Earth in the constellation of Orion, is truly remarkable, unexpected biologically, and its arising there is almost certainly unique in the Universe.

Its flame, small and dim by day, larger and brighter at night, attracts the mothlike "insects" (very different from Earth's arthropods) that supply the plant with protein. The flame also deters most predators, which would relish the lily's fleshy leaves or its thick, oily roots.

One has to marvel at how Natural Selection, powerful as it is, brought about this development. The verdict is not yet in, and biologists are still divided on the mechanism by which this Promethean plant managed to acquire and control fire. But it has and does! Imagine a mere plant rivaling man himself in such a triumph!

A stiff, narrow tube arises between the creamy petals with their black rosettes; from it comes hydrogen produced by electrolysis of water in the damp soil about the roots. The gas is set alight and burns continuously as circumstances permit.

Since pure hydrogen, as all chemistry students know, burns with almost no color, the lily actually infuses it with organic particles from its food, so that as with a candle, a yellow tinge makes it quite visible, especially in the dark. Energy to generate the hydrogen, as with insectivorous plants on Earth, comes from the bodies of its prey, which lured by the light are scorched, fall into a kind of bowl, and are absorbed and liquefied by acidic fluid secreted by the lily.

The most obvious question about this amazing organism, one of vital importance, is: How can any organic matter—in this case the tube—withstand fire and not be consumed and carbonized to ash? The answer is that the tube is lined with an oxide of silica plentiful in the soil of Vedius. On Earth, silicon fibers are found in many plants, like *Equisetum*, and even in some marine organisms.

Another crucial question is: How does the lily strike a light?

Saiph is a very hot star, and Vedius orbits it rather closely, so that sunlight, when available, is appreciable. In the morning, when dew forms on the plant, the light rays are focused by little globules of water collected by tentacles arising between the petals. It's astonishing to watch tiny points of light move slowly along the silica tube until, at the top, they meet, ignite the hydrogen, and flame appears. According to the legendary botanist, "The Female Darwin" Dr. (Exobiology) Susan Wright, who first studied the lily ninety years ago, tendrils bend gradually toward water drops collected on a weblike network, and thanks to surface tension, pick up globules and adjust the tiny magnifiers to exactly the right position to ignite the gas.

Of course, no plant has the kind of muscles common to animals, but as with our Venus Flytrap, it manages its movement by hydraulics, using sap.

For the Flame-Lily, wonderful as it is, life is not, pardon the phrase, a Bed of Roses. If its flame blows out when there are clouds, it cannot be lit; and, that night, predators move in, devour the leaves and destroy the plant. Even if missed by such enemies, a dark plant captures no insects.

An intriguing—some would say amusing—aspect of the strange plant is that in those rather uncommon areas fertile enough to sustain a small colony of flowers, a variety of little animals take advantage of their warmth by clustering there. It may be a symbiotic relationship, since these "squatters" have been known to unite to drive away the minor predators able to kill and feed upon the lily.

The plant is fairly rare even on Vedius. It is difficult to grow it on Earth, but plant fanciers in the small city of Pacific Grove, in California, have managed to accomplish that unusual feat. Be sure to go there and ask about them, if you can, as when you next visit Earth.

Bio-Balloons

Cayley, the fifth planet of the 1.9 magnitude binary star Beta Aurigae, 85 light years from Earth in the constellation Auriga, the Charioteer, named after the great Nineteenth Century algebraist, is home to the unique and almost inconceivable Montgolfier Plant.

According to the legendary Theodore L. Thau, one of the remarkable amateur botanists so oddly common in the period from 2269 to 2300, and author of the definitive biography of Susan Wright, the "Female Darwin," who studied the plant seventy-six years ago, the most amazing thing about the Montgolfier Plant is the way it solved the problem so vital to all of its kind—how to produce and disseminate, in highly adverse circumstances, enough viable seeds. That chore is especially difficult on Cayley, since its dense, cool atmosphere, mostly neon(!), with some oxygen, is totally windless below about ten kilometers, ruling out any possibility of dispersion by air currents as is common on Earth with maple seeds and others.

Another problem is that the kind of soil needed by the plant is rather rare, so it would do no good for it to shoot out seeds only a few feet as puffballs do on Earth; it requires somehow to send them a considerable distance in the hope they will land on suitable terrain for sprouting.

Let us see how brilliantly—no anthropomorphism intended—it beats the odds.

On maturing, the Montgolfier Plant produces, along with its normal, photosynthesizing leaves, two specialized kinds. One kind starts as tightly folded, very light, thin leaves, which then expand to form large (compared to the plant) balloons filled gradually with fairly heavy (compared to Cayley's atmosphere), complex, giant-moleculed organic gas that results from a complicated photosynthetic process which supplies the plant's basic energy.

These balloons, obviously, unlike those on Earth filled with hydrogen or helium, cannot ascend naturally, and that is why the second group of specialized leaves is required for Montgolfier's survival. These are also large: about 30 x 50 cm, concave, like bowls, and lined with a most unusual— for plants—membrane, thin and highly reflective. It is akin to the *tapetum lucidum* that causes the eyes of Earth's great cats to shine in near dark conditions.

When the twin suns of Beta Aurigae are high and hot, those reflective leaves, like little parabolic mirrors, direct the concentrated infrared energy on each balloon in turn, heating the enclosed gas so that the spheres, which carry seed pods from a thin stem at the base, rapidly ascend through the atmosphere until they reach the jet stream ten kilometers up! By the time the first balloon has entered the racing air, the second, depending on weather conditions, is soaring to join it. In a matter of about two hours, all the spheres have dispersed widely, dropping their seeds as they go. Truly a marvelous solution to a thorny problem!

Obviously this method of seed dispersal is very random, a most useful quality when good terrain is not easy to find. Further variability stems from the fact that according to the amount of heat and humidity in the jet stream, the little stems, each bearing a pod of exactly twenty-three seeds, dry out and break up at unpredictable intervals. Producing seeds is hard work for most plants, so it would be counter to its typical evolutionary function of using minimal energy should all twenty-three seeds hit the same spot on the ground. That contingency is also avoided by more random drying and other variables that cause the pods to tear open and scatter seeds well before they land. It should be noted that a healthy Montgolfier can live and repeatedly flower for as long as sixty years.

And, finally, lest I do not honor the men who first bore that name historically, the plant was named after the Montgolfier brothers, Joseph-Michel and Jacques-Étienne, who invented, built, and flew the first hot air balloon in France, on Earth, in 1782. Their balloon was made of paper, but dropped no seeds!

Botanical Justice

Watching a Jack Ketch Plant beginning its incredible food-gathering operation, even the most sophisticated, widely traveled exobotanist is bound to do a double take or even blink in disbelief at the sight.

That was surely the reaction of whoever first observed the amazing organism on the planet Stein of the 1.9 magnitude binary star Alpha Pavonis in the constellation Pavo, 180 light years from Earth, where the Jack Ketch proliferates as a weed over the whole southern hemisphere. The planet, Earthlike in many ways including size, was named for the brilliant Twenty Second Century mathematician, James D. Stein, Jr., whose proof of the famous Ptak-Alvarez Theorem, a notoriously thorny and difficult conjecture, firmly established the physics vital to modern starship propulsion systems.

But returning to the plant itself, what did that first observer actually see? From the plant's main stem, a sturdy one about three centimeters in diameter, a blue-green tendril sprouts and rapidly grows to a length of roughly twenty centimeters. It is eight millimeters wide, flexible, very tough, and quite slippery. As it matures, visibly lengthening, its pointed end waves about in an apparently random way at first, much like a branch of ivy exploring a wall, but then it finds exactly the right point in space from which to curl neatly about itself to form a perfect hangman's noose about ten centimeters in diameter, just the right size for the necks of those small, rodentlike animals on which the plant feeds, obtaining the nutrients missing in Stein's soil.

Just inside the dangling noose another tendril displays a fatty, fragrant nodule of cheeselike texture which is irresistible to many of the small animals that prowl the planet. When one such little hunter smells the bait and thrusts its head toward the attractive bud, a mechanism much like the one that snaps shut the leaves of Earth's Venus Flytrap jerks the noose violently upward, suspending and quickly strangling the prey.

An interesting aspect of the Jack Ketch Plant, named of course for England's generic hangman, is that the noose pulls its victim high enough above the ground so that it can't be garnered and taken away from the plant, so to speak, by other small predators for their own food.

Also quite innovative is the method by which the plant actually uses the animal it has so ingeniously noosed. In Stein's warm, humid, bacteria-rich climate decay sets in quickly, and the prey's rich juices dribble down to a porous, spongy leaf-base surrounding the plant's stem where it emerges from the ground. There, the nitrogen-rich fluid is absorbed and digested.

As might be inferred from the above description, the Jack Ketch is quite easy to grow on Earth, but that in itself does not assure its survival, since the cheesy bait, for some reason still unknown, not only doesn't attract terrestrial rodents or other possible food, but repels them. True, by attaching a bit of meat to the plant's attractant nodule, or by rubbing it with

18

chocolate, say, one can force the plant to catch mice and such, but few botanist/gardeners care to bother.

Redi's Squash Plant

Redi, the huge, only, planet of the orange giant Gamma Draconis, a 2.2 magnitude star in the constellation Draco, 154 light years from Earth, is home to the fascinating, unique Swatter Plant. The planet is named for the Seventeenth Century Italian naturalist, Francesco Redi, who by a series of brilliant experiments demolished the widely held but fallacious conviction that maggots arose spontaneously in rotting meat.

As for the plant itself, it was first spotted, oddly enough, not by a botanist, or even a biologist, but a mathematical philosopher, Edward J. Nauss, who was vacationing on Redi in 2348. Despite its size, some 100,000 kilometers in diameter, the planet, thanks to its low density, roughly that of lithium, has a surface gravity only slightly greater than Earth's, so that humans are perfectly comfortable there. That, plus a salubrious atmosphere and a host of interesting but non-aggressive animals, makes the planet terrestrial-friendly, so to speak.

The plant, which strikes many observers as almost clownish in its operations, thrives best in the fairly rare patches of soil that are rich in a very heavy, non-reactive, organic oil, almost twice the density of water. Water, which might serve the Swatter's needs tolerably well, is rare on Redi. Nitrogen is also in short supply, and since, like carbon and hydrogen, it is vital to a plant's survival, the plant must get it from living organisms much like our own insectivorous ones.

The basic operative parts of the Swatter consist of a large, 15 x 18 cm, base leaf, oval shaped, very porous, and covered with hundreds of trigger-hairs to detect and report any prey moving across it, and an upper leaf, to be described shortly. It should be noted that if too many such sensors are activated, the plant somehow knows the potential dinner is too big to be successfully attacked, and withholds its deadly blow. The base leaf, it should be pointed out, is dense and tough, almost as hard as wood, a quality essential to its role.

From the bottom of the Swatter's thick stem there springs a slender branch, highly flexible and vascular. It bears at its top, some fifty centimeters up as a rule, a structure, which, along with the base leaf, completes the plant's killing mechanism. It is roughly the same size as the "anvil" below, with a flat, tough lower side and a thinner, expansible upper one. The latter, when filled with the heavy oil drawn up by capillary and other forces common to Earth's plants, resembles a partly deflated balloon, flat on the bottom and shaped like half a football above.

Now, when any of the small, insectlike or even mouselike creatures numerous on Redi happen to traverse the base leaf, sensors alert the plant, which, like the Venus Flytrap on Earth, can free the oleo-draulic hammer instantly to fall. It was the *WHOMP!* of such a stroke that drew Nauss' attention and led to the discovery of the Swatter. He roared with laughter on realizing what that sound implied, so reminiscent it was of the ancient, primitive fly-swatters once common on Earth, and it led, of course, to the plant's name.

When the prey has been mashed against the firm base leaf, its juices are slowly absorbed by many little pores and digested for their nitrogen and other essential nutriments. Since the fluid-filled "balloon" is far too heavy to be hoisted back into position some fifty centimeters high, it is quickly drained of its oil by five valves evenly placed around its longer circumference and then raised by its springy, slender branch, after which it will gradually be refilled, ready for its next victim.

The Swatter is unique to Redi, but can be grown elsewhere if its vital oil, which has so far defied synthesis, is extracted from the ground and injected into foreign soil; but the operation is very tricky, and often fails. However, the experience of observing the plant's killing mechanism in operation is available in RNA tablet form in the gift shop in the north lobby.

Deadly Shade

Euler, the second planet of Alpha Crucis A, a 1.4 magnitude binary star, 321 light years from Earth, in the Crux constellation, is a bit like what our own moon will be millions of years in the future in that it always presents the same face to its primary. This means, of course, that one side is close to absolute zero in temperature, but the other quite warm under a strong, perpetual glare rich in ultraviolet and infrared radiation.

Its soil is lacking in some essential elements, notably phosphorus, so the plant I'm about to describe, one almost unbelievably unique in our galaxy, has to supplement its consequently rather inefficient method of photosynthesis by catching, killing, and absorbing some animal life, mainly the small, wormlike animals common in the narrow comfort zone bounding the sunlit hemisphere.

(The dark hemisphere supports no life but for strata of primitive bacterialike organisms deep under the surface.)

The key factor in sustaining the Deathshade Plant is the extremely thin atmosphere, which has the bare minimum of chlorine necessary for the plant's survival.

The Deathshade stands about a meter tall, has a dozen or so fairly typical leaves—which use sunlight to create silicon tetrachloride for the plant's

23

nourishment—but also has two other leaves that are quite different. One (a thick, spongy leaf with numerous sensors able to detect the passage of worms, which it does by its prey's body heat and motion) lies flat at the plant's base. The other, oversized, stiff, and thin, is held well up the stem and edgewise to the two suns.

Now, when a group of worms, which are numerous and far ranging on Euler's lit hemisphere and often travel in families of six or more, happen to cross the base leaf, and are tempted to sample its sweet secretions, the Deathshade responds, mechanically, at least, like Earth's Venus Flytrap, in that the big, edgewise leaf is suddenly snapped into a position perpendicular to the line of light.

In shade, in that very thin atmosphere, the temperature as on our moon or the dark side of Mercury, drops almost instantly to near absolute zero. The hapless worms, slow moving and not exactly quick witted, are stunned by the cold, and are literally frozen stiff in seconds.

Dead, they are then exposed again to the hot suns as the plant re-erects its deadly shade-leaf, after which bacteria, symbiotic with the plant, attack and liquefy the organisms so the plant can absorb their juices and obtain the elements it needs to survive, the elements the worms concentrate in their bodies as they have burrowed through what passes for soil.

Oddly, the Deathshade can easily be grown on Earth in a large chamber filled with chlorine gas and evacuated to about thirty millimeters of pressure. A roof transparent to sunlight will be needed, of course, and a few inches of proper silicon soil in which to root a seedling. As the plant matures, frozen chewable vitamin pills are placed on the base leaf, and the

Deathshade absorbs, and is very happy to get, the microscopic amounts of phosphorus and other useful minerals. The light of Earth's sun, if not as powerful as that of Alpha Crucis A, is adequate for photosynthesis.

I have to marvel at this amazing killing machine, which instead of using aggression, succeeds by subtracting that which its prey needs to live, namely warmth. It's as if one could catch a fish on Earth not by pulling it from the water, but by somehow draining the water away from the fish!

Executioner Plant

The Executioner Plant, found on the planet Wiles, named after the brilliant Twentieth Century mathematician (who in 1995, finalized his very long, thorny proof of Fermat's Last Theorem), the sixth of the star Beta Puppis, an inconceivable 2,400 light years from Earth, might well have been called a botanical San Quentin, after the quaint California prison, where, centuries ago, condemned criminals were put to death in a way eerily similar to the method used by this strange shrub on its prey.

It's a short, bulky plant, which, unlike many of the others I've described in this series, has only one specialized leaf; all that it needs, as you'll see. It hangs from a springy branch, concave side down, and resembles the top of an umbrella. It measures about thirty centimeters across its opening and hangs about that high above the ground.

When one of the small, mouselike animals passes under that living hood, it drops over the prey with a speed suggestive of the Venus Flytrap snapping shut. Apparently, the animal's body heat, as it rises, alerts small, very sensitive areas on the leaf's inner surface and that leads to the dropping of the deadly hood.

That is not so remarkable in itself and the plant could, given a little time—since the hood makes a fairly tight seal with the ground—kill its victim by simple suffocation. But the Executioner Plant has a better, faster way of dispatching its hapless prey. Once the leaf-hood is firmly in contact with the soil, the plant releases inside the container two or three hard pods, each the size of a cherry stone, but more friable.

Like peach pits, they contain rather large concentrations of a cyanide salt, which, on reaching the moist, acidic soil of Wiles, react by releasing substantial amounts of hydrogen cyanide gas, quickly killing the trapped animal. As a further contribution to the Executioner's survival, that kind of soil attacks and liquefies organic matter in moments, after which the plant's roots, a few centimeters deep, can absorb the vital nourishment.

After about thirty minutes, depending on the size of its catch, the plant lifts its hood, ready for another victim. Very probably, it could raise the hood more quickly, but why expose its meal to some other predator any sooner than it must?

The Executioner was discovered only recently, since even with our most advanced scouting ships and the wonderful new warp drive just developed by Beverly Power and Wallace Granstrom at BIT, 2,400 light years is a most daunting distance indeed.

Only one Executioner was brought back to Earth (that was a year ago) and whether it will live much longer is problematical. It can be found in the Exobotanical Garden on the large island in the archipelago of Monterey, off the new coast of California.

Wheel in the Sky

After giving you readers brief summaries of some truly astonishing plants, I'm often asked which of the many botanical marvels I've researched I consider most amazing.

It's not an easy question, but yet I would unhesitatingly answer: it is the one plant which actually grows and uses a wheel, something even higher creatures do not always discover, relying instead on sledges, travoises, or the backs of various strong, patient, and agile domesticated beasts of burden.

I refer, of course, to the incredible bush called the Holy Roller, which is found only on the second planet of Gamma Velorum A in the constellation Vela, a binary star system with a magnitude of 1.8 and located a staggering 840 light years from Earth.

Now, if one were to ask professional botanists (as I did concerning the Flame-Lily, another unbelievable organism) to come up with a biologically plausible way a plant could grow and employ a wheel, few of them would be able to supply a credible answer. In fact, it boggles even the most agile mind to conceive of such a development; yet the Holy Roller's solution, like so many great breakthroughs in nature and in all fields of science, is dazzlingly simple.

What it does is to sprout a large, woody, stiff, circular leaf which is reinforced by fibers of lignin and silicon like those found in Earth's *Equisetum* horsetail or scouring rush. Now, as the leaf matures and hardens to form a disc-wheel, the really tricky part is how to detach from the plant so that it is free to rotate, yet not just fall off.

Well, consider the budding area, a thick, tough nodule, hollow inside, and at the center of the round leaf, its break-off point, a solid, slightly smaller ball that is just too large to escape its container in the plant's stem. In short, it can revolve, but can't pull free. It is clearly a wheel, if a crude one plagued by friction, but adequate for the Holy Roller's need.

Driven by the planet's strong, regular winds, the plant, withdrawing its shallow roots, rolls easily on three or more of its wheels across the vast plains.

Why it must do so is also interesting. The planet (still unnamed, with a battle going on between those who want to call it Crick and others who favor Watson) is very short of water, which appears only in small, shallow pools and some underground deposits that are barely more than moist … so by ranging widely, the Holy Roller seeks and finds a little pool in which to extend its roots. The scant amount of water is quickly absorbed, and the plant may have time to reproduce before rolling off in search of another puddle.

It should be noted that although the plant's name seems to derive from its unique mode of travel, another factor is the fact that its purple, fleshy flowers are cross-shaped.

It was first seen in 2552 (Gregorian calendar) by Professor Jack Arnold, who pursued a specimen across several miles of flatlands expecting—even anticipating, with a vision of fame—to find an intelligent "driver" of what was obviously a vehicle with wheels. Although disappointed on realizing the only driver was the wind, he also understood what an astounding plant he had run down; not a bad consolation prize!

It was hoped, for a time, that such a plant might survive and flourish on some of Earth's deserts, but unfortunately they are either always bone-dry, or periodically inundated by flashfloods, neither condition suitable for the survival of a Holy Roller, which for such a mobile plant is quite set in its ways and requirements.

A few will grow in confinement, i.e. botanical gardens, but have to be cautiously watered and obviously must be staked down, disallowed to roll freely, for, faced with an obstacle—lacking short-term problem solving ability—they bump and bump futilely until worn to a frazzle.

Too bad; they are beautiful.

About the Author

Arthur Porges was born in Chicago, Illinois on August 20, 1915. One of four brothers, he was educated at Roosevelt High School and Senn High School before enrolling at The Lewis Institute where he achieved a Bachelor of Science Degree in Mathematics. After the successful completion of his postgraduate studies, through which he attained Masters Degrees in Mathematics and Engineering from the Illinois Institute of Technology, Porges enlisted in the U.S. Army in 1942. During the Second World War he served as an artillery instructor, teaching algebra and trigonometry to field personnel. He was stationed at various military installations including Camp White in Oregon, Fort Sill, Oklahoma, Camp Roberts, California and at Barnes Hospital in Vancouver, Washington. After the war Porges returned to Illinois and taught mathematics at the Western Military Academy, going on to serve as an assistant professor at De Paul University. Having taught at Occidental College in Los Angeles for a brief stint in the late forties, Porges made a permanent move to California in 1951 and spent several years as a mathematics teacher at Los Angeles City College. During this period he wrote and sold short stories as a sideline. In 1957, Porges retired from teaching to write full-time. He went on to publish hundreds of short stories in numerous magazines and newspapers. Many of his stories appeared in *Alfred Hitchcock's Mystery Magazine*, *Ellery Queen's Mystery Magazine*, *Amazing Stories* and *The Magazine of Fantasy and*

Science Fiction. His fiction spanned several genres, with tales ranging from science fiction and fantasy to horror, mysteries, and so on. At his most prolific his work was appearing in three or four periodicals in one month alone. Among his best-known stories are "The Ruum," "The Rats," "No Killer Has Wings," "The Mirror" and "The Rescuer." Ten previous book collections of his short stories have been published: *Three Porges Parodies and a Pastiche* (1988), *The Mirror and Other Strange Reflections* (2002), *Eight Problems in Space: The Ensign De Ruyter Stories* (2008), *The Adventures of Stately Homes and Sherman Horn* (2008), *The Calabash of Coral Island and Other Early Stories* (2008), *The Miracle of the Bread and Other Stories* (2008), *The Devil and Simon Flagg and Other Fantastic Tales* (2009), *The Curious Cases of Cyriack Skinner Grey* (2009), *The Ruum and Other Science Fiction Stories* (2010) and *The Rescuer and Other Science Fiction* Stories (2014). A keen birdwatcher and an avid reader, in later years Porges wrote many articles, essays and poems, most of which were published in the *Monterey Herald.* Several of his poems were collected in the book *Spring, 1836: Selected Poems* (2008). After spells in Laguna Beach and San Clemente, Porges moved north, eventually settling in Pacific Grove. He passed away, at the age of 90, in May 2006.

A Checklist of Science Fiction

Note: The following checklist contains all the stories Arthur Porges wrote in the science fiction genre by chronological order of first publication. Further information on where individual stories were reprinted in anthologies and book collections is available online at: http://arthurporges.atwebpages.com.

"The Rats"
Man's World, February 1951

"The Fly"
The Magazine of Fantasy and Science Fiction, September 1952

"Story Conference"
The Magazine of Fantasy and Science Fiction, May 1953

"The Ruum"
The Magazine of Fantasy and Science Fiction, October 1953

"The Unwilling Professor"
Dynamic Science Fiction, January 1954

"By a Fluke"
The Magazine of Fantasy and Science Fiction, October 1955

"The Logic of Rufus Weir"
The Magazine of Fantasy and Science Fiction,
November 1955

"Guilty as Charged"
The New York Post, November 27th, 1955

"The Entity"
Fantastic Universe, December 1955

"Emergency Operation"
The Magazine of Fantasy and Science Fiction, May
1956

"Whirlpool"
Fantastic Universe, March 1957

"A Touch of Sun" (written with Irwin Porges)
Fantastic, April 1959

"Security"
Amazing Stories, September 1959

"Off His Rocker"
Fantastic, February 1960

"A Specimen for the Queen" (sequel to "The Ruum")
The Magazine of Fantasy and Science Fiction, May
1960

"The Auto Hawks"
Amazing Stories, September 1960

"The Melanas"
Fantastic, December 1960

"The Radio"
Fantastic, December 1960

"Degree Candidate" (as by Peter Arthur)
Fantastic, January 1961

"Revenge"
Amazing Stories, February 1961

"Mulberry Moon"
Fantastic, April 1961

"The Rescuer"
Analog, July 1962

"The Topper" (a Dr. Corman story)
Analog, February 1963

"The Formula" (a Dr. Corman story)
Amazing Stories, July 1963

"Controlled Experiment" (a Dr. Corman story)
Analog, August 1963

"Problem Child"
Analog, April 1964

"Alien"
Rascal, September 1964

"Urned Reprieve" (an Ensign De Ruyter story)
Amazing Stories, October 1964

"Irresistible Attraction"
Rascal, November 1964

"The Moths"
Amazing Stories, December 1964

"The Fanatic"
Fantastic, December 1964

"Wheeler Dealer" (an Ensign De Ruyter story)
Amazing Stories, March 1965

"Ensign De Ruyter: Dreamer" (an Ensign De Ruyter story)
Amazing Stories, April 1965

"The Good Seed" (an Ensign De Ruyter story)
Amazing Stories, August 1965

"Turning Point"
The Magazine of Fantasy and Science Fiction, September 1965

"Dusty Answer" (an Ensign De Ruyter story)
Amazing Stories, October 1965

"A Civilized Community"
Bizarre! Mystery Magazine, October 1965

"Pressure" (an Ensign De Ruyter story)
Amazing Stories, February 1966

"Priceless Possession"
Galaxy, June 1966

"The Dragons of Tesla" (an Ensign De Ruyter story)
Fantastic, October 1968

"Vedius Flame-Lily" (Unusual Plants of the Galaxy)
Memo, ca. 1996

"Bio-Balloons" (Unusual Plants of the Galaxy)
Memo, ca. 1996

"Botanical Justice" (Unusual Plants of the Galaxy)
Memo, ca. 1996

"Redi's Squash Plant" (Unusual Plants of the Galaxy)
Memo, Issue 64, ca. 1996

"Deadly Shade" (Unusual Plants of the Galaxy)
Memo, Issue 70, ca. 1996

"Executioner Plant" (Unusual Plants of the Galaxy)
Memo, Issue 74, ca. 1996

"Wheel in the Sky" (Unusual Plants of the Galaxy)
Memo, ca. 1996

"Movie Show"
The Magazine of Fantasy and Science Fiction,
February 1999

"Luz"
The Magazine of Fantasy and Science Fiction, May
2003

"By the Light of Day"
The Magazine of Fantasy and Science Fiction, June
2004

"Brain Slug" (an Ensign De Ruyter story)
Eight Problems in Space: The Ensign De Ruyter Stories, The Battered Silicon Dispatch Box, 2008

"No Survivors"
The Calabash of Coral Island and Other Early Stories, Richard Simms Publications, 2008

"The Terror of the Mindanao Depths"
The Calabash of Coral Island and Other Early Stories, Richard Simms Publications, 2008

"Denizens of the Drop"
The Calabash of Coral Island and Other Early Stories, Richard Simms Publications, 2008

"Monsters of the Grasslands"
The Calabash of Coral Island and Other Early Stories, Richard Simms Publications, 2008

"Night of the Puppet"
The Miracle of the Bread and Other Stories, Richard Simms Publications, 2008

"The Mannering Report"
The Ruum and Other Science Fiction Stories, Richard Simms Publications, 2010

"Doomsday Incident"
The Rescuer and Other Science Fiction Stories, Richard Simms Publications, 2014

www.ingramcontent.com/pod-product-compliance
Lightning Source LLC
Chambersburg PA
CBHW071226130626
46555CB00004B/1861